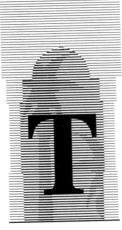

T H E
FRIENDS
of the
Beverly Hills
Public Library

A JUST FOR A DAY BOOK

JAGUAR IN THE RAIN FOREST

JOANNE RYDER

ILLUSTRATED BY

MICHAEL ROTHMAN

MORROW JUNIOR BOOKS / NEW YORK

The author gratefully acknowledges the research of Dr. Alan Rabinowitz, author of *Jaguar* (Arbor House, 1986), and thanks him for his expert reading of this manuscript. His scientific work brought attention to the plight of jaguars and contributed to the establishment of the world's first jaguar refuge, the Cockscomb Basin Forest Reserve, in Belize, Central America.

AUTHOR'S NOTE

The jaguar *(Panthera onca)* is the largest cat in the Americas and the third largest on earth. Until this century jaguars lived in the southern U.S. Now found only in Central and South America, they are uncommon except in remaining patches of protected or uninhabited forest.

Jaguars have been hunted for their distinctive fur. No two jaguars have exactly the same pattern of dark spots and ringlike rosettes. Sport killing and habitat destruction have also decreased their numbers.

Jaguars' muscular bodies; powerful jaws; sharp, retractable claws; and keen senses make them strong hunters. They will stalk or ambush any available prey—wild pigs, capybaras, deer, fish, turtles, and caiman. When larger prey is scarce, small, numerous prey, such as armadillos, must make up the bulk of their diet. The name *jaguar* is believed to come from a South American Indian word meaning "the wild beast that can kill its prey in a single bound."

Jaguars hunt alone and within their own territories. To mark the boundaries of its home range, a jaguar may leave visual scraping signs as well as scent markings. Its distinctive deep grunting roar may also announce its presence to other jaguars.

Though active day or night, jaguars seem most active after sunset and before dawn. While they can climb well, they do not hunt in the trees, like smaller cats, but on the forest floor. Excellent swimmers, they often are found near rivers and streams where they and their prey come to drink.

While jaguars live in a variety of habitats, the tropical rain forests of Central and South America provide them with abundant prey, shelter, and seclusion. The rain forest habitat and creatures illustrated in this book are ones typical of French Guiana.

Acrylic paint was used for the full-color illustrations. The text type is 14-point ITC Garamond Book.

Text copyright © 1996 by Joanne Ryder. Illustrations copyright © 1996 by Michael Rothman. All rights reserved.
No part of this book may be reproduced or utilized in any form or by any means, electronic or mechanical, including photocopying, recording, or by any information storage and retrieval system, without permission in writing from the Publisher. Inquiries should be addressed to William Morrow and Company, Inc., 1350 Avenue of the Americas, New York, NY 10019.

Printed in Singapore at Tien Wah Press.
1   2   3   4   5   6   7   8   9   10

Library of Congress Cataloging-in-Publication Data
Ryder, Joanne.   Jaguar in the rain forest / Joanne Ryder; illustrations by Michael Rothman.   p. cm.—(A Just for a day book)
Summary: The reader spends a day as a jaguar, experiencing the life of this rain forest animal.
ISBN 0-688-12990-0 (trade)—ISBN 0-688-12991-9 (library)   1. Jaguar—Juvenile fiction.   [1. Jaguar—Fiction.   2. Rain forests—Fiction.]
I. Rothman, Michael, ill.   II. Title.   III. Series.   PZ10.3.R954Jag 1995   [E]—dc20   94-16646   CIP AC

Imagine
you are climbing
a ragged tree trunk
hand over hand.
You are speckled
in sunlight
that warms you
and changes you
till...

You are climbing
higher and higher
paw over paw,
gripping with
curved claws.
You are larger
and stronger than ever,
covered in fur—
golden fur,
speckled with
a dark pattern
all your own.

On this hot day,
you stretch
and lie relaxed,
blending within
the speckled sunlight.
You are a jaguar
in the rain forest,
hidden within
a green world
of dangling vines
and towering trees.
As you lie,
only the tip
of your tail
twitches alertly,
only your ears
flick away
dark flies buzzing
around you.

High in the treetops,
long-armed spider monkeys
swing between branches.
You look up,
your sensitive ears
twisting, tracing
the monkeys moving by.
Your golden eyes
keenly search
the giant trees
that stretch toward
brilliant sunlight,
where birds soar,
flowers bloom,
and butterflies glide
in their world
beyond your reach.

You are a jaguar,
and your world
lies below.
Climb down, jaguar,
jump down
to the forest floor,
where trees begin
and rivers run,
ever moving
to the sea.

You tuck your claws
inside your paws
and walk
along the river,
leaving a trail
of deep paw prints
in the wet sand.
The last rays
of sunlight dance
on the flowing river,
dance on your
golden, speckled fur.
Warm and thirsty,
you drink,
your tongue curling,
lapping fresh water.

You are a jaguar
crossing the river
at the end of day,
swimming boldly
with powerful paws,
the tip of your tail
waving high and dry.

All around you,
the forest fades
from green to gray.
In the grayness,
tired creatures
seek shelter and sleep.
Others wake
to creep and climb
and glide and fly
within the dark forest.
This is a good time
to hunt, jaguar.

You hear
the booming calls
of howler monkeys
ending their day,
the haunting
echoes of unseen frogs
awakening night.
And you
roar and roar—
your voice
deep and loud—
Uh! Uh! Uh! Uh! Uh!
In the dark forest
you hunt,
roaring and
leaving signs
so other jaguars know
you are here,
this place
is yours now.

In the darkness
your eyes change—
black pupils grow wider—
catching and reflecting
light so you can see
the small ones
who wake now
looking for
nuts and fruit,
fallen treasures
lying on the ground.
You are a hunter
moving so carefully,
so slowly and quietly,
no one can see you.

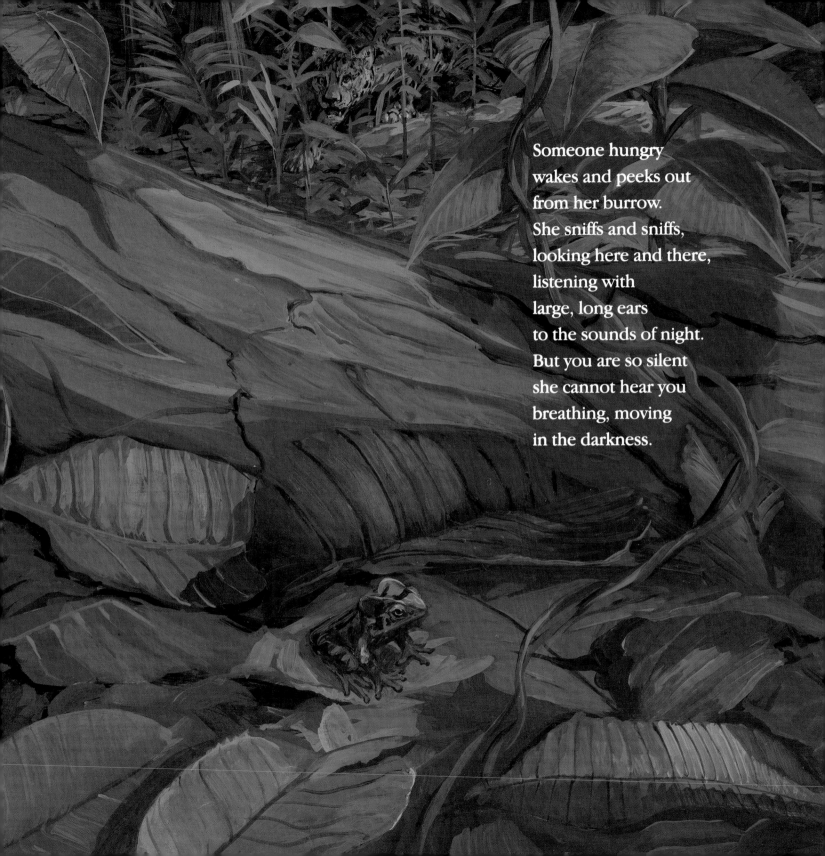

Someone hungry
wakes and peeks out
from her burrow.
She sniffs and sniffs,
looking here and there,
listening with
large, long ears
to the sounds of night.
But you are so silent
she cannot hear you
breathing, moving
in the darkness.

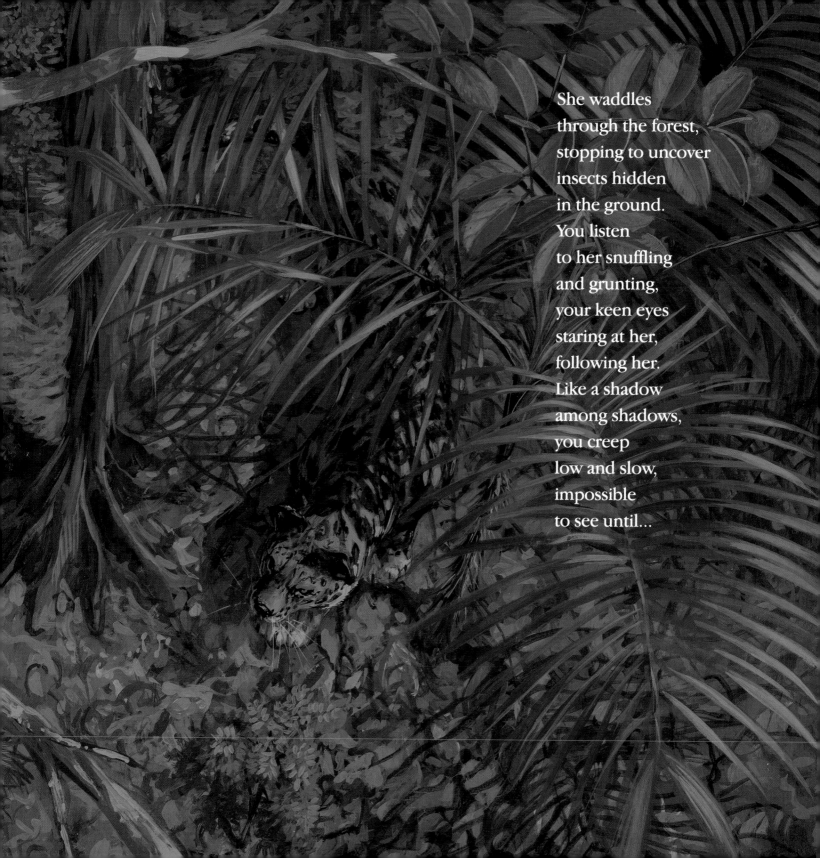

She waddles
through the forest,
stopping to uncover
insects hidden
in the ground.
You listen
to her snuffling
and grunting,
your keen eyes
staring at her,
following her.
Like a shadow
among shadows,
you creep
low and slow,
impossible
to see until...

You leap!
In one bound
you reach
armadillo,
your strong legs
never touching
the ground
until you
have caught her
with your
large paws,
sharp claws,
and powerful jaws.

In a grassy
sheltered place,
you eat,
then lick
yourself clean,
your rough tongue
combing your fur.
Then you rest,
lying on
the forest floor.

You are a jaguar
in the night,
listening to
the sky roar
over your head
and raindrops drum
on your leafy roof.
In this forest
rain brings life
to plants and trees
and all who
live within
its greenness.
You feel
the raindrops
landing on
your furry back,
your whiskered face,
changing you
till...

You are home again,
snug and dry,
sheltered from
the rain falling,
thunder booming
in the distance.
And you dream
of a forest
hot and wet
where monkeys swing,
bats flutter,
and jaguars roar
free and wild.